W9-AGU-662

THE BIG BIKE RACE

THE BIG BIKE RACE

Lucy Jane Bledsoe

drawings by Sterling Brown

Harcourt

Orlando   Boston   Dallas   Chicago   San Diego

Visit *The Learning Site!*

www.harcourtschool.com

This edition is published by special arrangement with Holiday House, Inc.

Grateful acknowledgment is made to Holiday House, Inc.
for permission to reprint *The Big Bike Race* by Lucy Jane Bledsoe,
illustrated by Sterling Brown. Text copyright © 1995 by Lucy Jane Bledsoe;
illustrations copyright © 1995 by Sterling Brown.

Printed in the United States of America

ISBN   0-15-314372-X

3   4   5   6   7   8   9   10   060   03   02

For my favorite young people in the world:
Emily, Andrew, Krista, Anna, Kelsey, Marion,
and Celine

1: The Birthday Present

Ernie Peterson flew out of bed on his tenth birthday. He landed squarely on his feet. He swung his head around, looking hard. He did not see, at least not right there in his bedroom, a racing bike.

He sat back down on his bed and sighed. Although it was early June and only eight in the morning, it was already hot and muggy. With a fast bike, though, he could speed through the heat and make his own breeze.

Ernie wanted a silver racing bike with red handlebars. He wanted one of those light, streamlined bikes, the kind with the thin, pointed seats. He could just feel his hands in the curve of the handlebars. He could just feel the smooth turning of the pedals. Maybe his dream bike was waiting for him in the kitchen.

Ernie dressed quickly.

Ernie Peterson lived in Washington, D.C. That happened to be the same city in which the president and other important lawmakers lived. Ernie hoped that some of the greatness of the city might rub off on him.

"Delusions of grandeur!" his grandma had said last week when he pointed this out to her. But his grandma had no imagination. That was her main problem. She was always one hundred percent practical.

Of course, Ernie knew he lived all the way across town from the president. And the apartment he shared with his sister and grandma was a bit smaller than the White House. But it was no less grand. At least not in Ernie's eyes.

Hadn't President Lincoln grown up in a log cabin? Well, then.

He looked at the magazine pictures tacked up over his bed. There was Magic Johnson, M.C. Hammer, and Martin Luther King, Jr. (his grandma had put that one up). As far as Ernie knew, none of those guys were *born* famous.

Ernie decided that now was the time to start working on someday becoming famous. After all, today was his tenth birthday, his first two-digit year.

He would begin by using his full name. From now on, he would go by "Ernest." He wished he could add "sir" or "the third" to his name, but that wouldn't be honest. His father's name had been Carl. And practical Grandma was very big on honesty.

Ernie—or rather, Ernest—faced his bedroom mirror. He began to practice being great. He spoke to the mirror, pretending to be a spokesperson for the president.

"Sir Ernest Peterson the third, sir? I hear you're the fastest bike racer in the world. The president would like to see you."

Ernest bowed to the mirror. He began to answer himself. But, too late, he saw his sister's face appear in the doorway. As usual, Sniffy, her small brown-and-white dog, scampered around her ankles.

"Grandma," Melissa screamed, just like an eight-year-old, "Ernie's talking to himself!"

"Get lost," said Ernest. Then he stormed to the kitchen after Melissa and her mutt. He said, "What we need in this family is a *man*."

"Delusions of grandeur!" Melissa cried.

"You don't even know what that means," Ernest accused.

Melissa only laughed. Ernest thought

(4)

her laugh was like a sick monkey's. Her voice came out in high sharp notes. Sniffy barked along with her.

For once their grandma didn't take Melissa's side, probably on account of it being Ernest's birthday. She said, "That's enough, Melissa. We're waiting on you to be the man around here, Ernie. That's your job."

Ernest wanted to continue making smart comments. But he caught sight of the big bowl of dark, gooey chocolate in front of his grandma. He closed his mouth. She must be making a birthday cake. Then he remembered his bike. He looked quickly around the kitchen. No bike.

His excitement dropped like a rock off a cliff. Besides the cake batter, there was not a sign of his birthday to be seen.

Ernest sat quietly at the table and ate his eggs and toast. Whenever he felt disappointed, he thought about his parents. He didn't really remember anything about them. From pictures, he knew that his mother wore her hair in a short Afro and his father wore a neat mustache. Both his parents were tall like he was. He was sure that *they* would have gotten him a bike for his birthday.

All year long he'd dropped big hints to his grandma about the bike he wanted. He knew she didn't have a lot of money. But for once, couldn't she give up on being practical?

After all, look what Melissa got for *her* birthday! For months Melissa talked about wanting a puppy. Finally, his grandma found a free one. A little girl was giving them away in front of the grocery store. It even had all its shots.

Well! Ernest thought hotly. Maybe Sniffy came free at first. But with all the food that dog ate, they could have bought him *three* bikes. Besides, what can you do with a dog in the city? A bike was a whole lot more practical than that.

(6)

The Birthday Present

Sometimes Ernest thought that had his parents lived, they wouldn't have been so poor. At the time of the accident, his mother had been in medical school and his father had just opened his own auto parts shop. They had taken out loans for the school and business, so that when they were killed in the car accident, there was no money left.

"Finish your breakfast," his grandma said. Ernest lowered his head near his plate. He felt bad for having such selfish thoughts. Especially the part about not having enough money. Grandma worked hard to take care of Melissa and him.

When Ernest had almost finished eating, his grandma said, "I've got something to show you, Ernie."

"It's Ernest now, Grandma," Ernest said. Then he wished he hadn't. She gave him one of her long cool looks. Those looks usually meant he had gone too far with something. But now she just shook her head (probably because it was his birthday) and said, "Come here."

Ernest pushed the last of his toast in his mouth. Then he followed Melissa and their grandma to her room. There, in the middle of the rug, was a huge, awkward-looking object covered with a big white sheet.

Ernest was so excited he couldn't swallow his toast. It stuck on the way down, and he began choking. Both his grandma and Melissa pounded him on the back until he stopped.

"Go ahead," his grandma said. She didn't smile often, but now she grinned widely. "Pull off that sheet."

Ernest walked toward the sheet like a cat creeping up on a mouse. He moved slowly and carefully. He circled around it once. Then he took a corner of the sheet. Like a magician, he yanked it away in one movement.

Ernest's heart sank. There sat a huge, clunky, *yellow* bike. The seat was broad and flat. The wheels were fat. The handlebars did not curl under like a racing bike. They were wide, thick, and sturdy. Hanging off the ends of the handlebars were colorful streamers. Baskets were attached on either side of the back wheel. The fenders and frame were rusted in places. Worst of all, there was a little bell on the handlebars.

The secondhand bike was, above all else, one hundred percent practical.

Ernest sucked in his breath. This was his birthday. And his grandma spent her money to get him something she thought he'd love.

"Gee, Grandma," Ernest said, "it's . . . uh, just what I wanted."

His grandma beamed her biggest smile. She said, "I had those baskets put on so you could pick things up for me at the store."

Ernest wanted to die. How could he ride around the neighborhood on this thing? What would his friends say?

The Birthday Present

He'd soon find out because his grandma said, "Go on out and try it. While you're at it, pick up some butter for your birthday dinner."

"Maybe I'll wait awhile," Ernest tried.

"Go on!" his grandma said. "I need the butter."

Ernest shook his head. Then he wheeled the big ugly bike out the apartment door.

2: The Bike Crash

"What is *that*, Ernie?" Mike and Jack closed in on Ernest.

"Listen, fellows, the name's Ernest now, OK?" Ernest tried to speak in his most presidential voice. "And this bike you see is the newest thing in all the bike shops. Yep. You'll both want to trade your bikes in for one."

Ernest's plan didn't work. Mike and Jack burst out laughing. Jack pulled on the streamers hanging from the handlebars. "This looks like a two-year-old's bike!"

Mike put a foot in one of the side baskets. "What are these for? Your little sister and her dog?"

"OK. OK." Ernest held up his hand to quiet his friends. "You're right. I wasn't honest with you. This bike is not the newest thing in bikes. This bike, my friends, was given to me by the White House. You see, I have a new job with the Secret Service. I'll be delivering top secret, highly important papers. That's what the baskets are for."

Ernest leaned on his bike and looked over his friends' faces. They seemed to buy the story for about, well, one second. Then Jack said, "Quit lying, Ernie. You got this silly-looking bike for your birthday."

"I told you once," Ernest yelled, jumping on his bike, "from now on, to you guys, it's Ernest."

Ernest raced away from his laughing

friends. Already he could hear them telling all the guys in their school class this fall about his bike with the baskets and streamers. What a dumb, dumb bike. And he'd have to ride it every day if he didn't want to break his grandma's heart.

Ernest rode fast and hard to get over being upset. He thought that if he went fast enough, his bike would be a big blur. That way people he passed couldn't laugh. Ernest forgot all about his grandma's butter.

Before he knew it, he passed the White House. He stopped for a moment to see if the president was on the lawn. He wasn't.

Maybe someday, he thought, I'll be the first African-American president of the United States, and Mike and Jack will be sorry they didn't show me more respect. No sooner had he thought that than he could hear his grandma's voice saying, "Delusions of grandeur!"

Ernest climbed back on his bike. Just then a skinny but muscular man tore by on a beautiful racing bike. Ernest didn't often see black guys on racing bikes. The man wore a biking helmet, biking shoes, and those tight racing shorts. He also had a shirt with special pockets in the back. A Powerbar stuck out of one of the pockets. Ernest knew bike racers ate lots of high-energy health foods.

Ernest rose up off the seat of his bike. He pedaled madly. He wanted to see if he could keep up with the man.

In the next moment, Ernest saw a big delivery truck pull in front of the biker. The biker yelled, "Watch out!" He squeezed his brakes. Too late, though. His front wheel struck the back of the truck. The biker sailed off his bike and landed on the sidewalk. The bike lay on the street like a dead animal.

With all the traffic noise, and the size of the delivery truck, the trucker didn't even know the biker had hit him. He kept on driving.

Ernest rushed over to help the biker. He laid his own clunky bike down on the sidewalk. Then he pulled the racing bike out of the street so it wouldn't get any more damaged. By then, the young man was sitting up on the sidewalk rubbing his knee.

"You OK?" Ernest asked.

The man shook his head angrily. "Those truckers don't look where they're going." He pointed to his bike. "Do you know how much I paid for that bike?" He put his head in his hands as if he would cry.

"No," Ernest said almost in a whisper, "how much?"

The man looked up at Ernest but didn't answer. He dragged himself to his feet. Then his eye caught Ernest's bike and the man cracked a smile. "That is the silliest-looking bicycle I've ever seen."

Ernest wanted to die. He was about to say it wasn't his. But the biker picked it up off the ground and looked it over carefully. He laughed softly to himself. "Listen," the biker finally said to him, "my name's Sonny. I'm several miles from home. I'm going to lock up what's left of my bike. Think you could give me a lift home on this thing?"

Ernest's eyes widened. He looked over the racer's strong legs. He looked over his cool riding clothes again. Ernest couldn't believe that this racer would be caught dead on his yellow bike.

The racer must have read his thoughts. "Hey, kid, there's nothing wrong with this bike. For one, there's less chance it will get stolen in the city. Get a fancy bike, and someone rips it off first thing. This is a perfectly good machine. Come on. Climb on behind me. I'll show you what I mean."

Sonny locked up his mangled bike on a nearby fence. Then he got on Ernest's bike and stood straddling the bar. Ernest climbed on the seat behind him. He held onto Sonny's shirt. Sonny started riding standing up. The bike was a little small for

(17)

him, but not that much. Sonny was short while Ernest was tall. Sonny's strong legs made even this bike move out fast.

They tore past the White House. Ernest waved to the president—in case he was looking out the window.

They raced down one street after another. It surprised Ernest to see they were approaching his own neighborhood—and so quickly. In a second, Sonny turned right down his street!

Up ahead Ernest saw Mike and Jack sitting on the steps. Ernest and Sonny flew by like the wind. Ernest waved and laughed at their shocked faces. Mike's and Jack's mouths hung open like fly traps.

Finally, Sonny pulled over on the next street. "Here's where I live. I'll get my car and take you home."

"That won't be necessary," Ernest told him. "We're neighbors!" He put out a hand and Sonny shook it. "I live one street over. My name's Ernest Peterson the third."

Ernest looked at the ground. He felt a little shy lying about his name. But it didn't hurt anything.

Sonny smiled. "Thanks for the ride, Ernest." Sonny winked. "That is, *Sir* Ernest Peterson the third."

"Hey," Ernest said softly as Sonny entered his apartment building, "I didn't even tell him about the 'Sir.'"

Ernest looked at his yellow bike. He felt as if some magic had just disappeared in thin air. Moments ago his bike had been a racehorse. It had been a magic carpet. It had been a jet. Now, once again, it was as plain and ordinary as could be.

Ernest hopped back on and rode home.

Jack and Mike were now throwing a football in the street. "Hey, who was that?" Mike asked.

Ernest saw the boys' eyes shining with envy. He thought he'd just ignore his friends for now. He brushed past them and went inside.

(20)

The Bike Crash

Ernest found his grandma glowering at him. The butter!

"I'm going to get it now, Grandma!" Ernest said, but she caught him by the tail of his shirt.

"If it weren't your birthday, I'd tan your hide. Gone three hours, late for lunch, and no butter."

Ernest slunk off to wash his hands. He felt like Sniffy when he put his tail between his legs.

What a birthday!

Well, it hadn't been all bad. He had met Sonny, a real bike racer.

3: Getting a Coach

Ernest didn't take his bike out again for a week. When his grandma asked him to pick up something at the store, he walked. When he needed to go farther away, he took the bus.

Ernest noticed that his grandma didn't say a word about the bike. He didn't want to hurt her feelings. Yet he just couldn't bring himself to take it out.

On Saturday morning, Ernest picked up the sports page. The headline read, BIKE

Getting a Coach

RACERS TRAIN FOR THE CITYWIDE CUP. Ernest read the story.

The Citywide Cup was the most important bike race in Washington, D. C. The story said that a man named Tiger Jones was expected to win this year. The story named several other strong racers. At the end of the list was the name, "Sonny King."

That had to be the same Sonny! thought Ernest.

Ernest read the story all the way to the end. There, at the very bottom, was a list of all the races in the Citywide Cup. Ernest saw that there was a race for juniors, ten- to twelve-year-olds. And the prize . . . a racing bike!

Ernest's thoughts took off like a dog after a rabbit. How could he enter that race? Could he use the big yellow clunker? Didn't Sonny say it was a perfectly good machine?

But Ernest didn't know much about bike racing. He needed help.

Ernest flew off the couch and went for his bike. He stopped in the kitchen and asked his grandma, "Want me to stop at the store today?"

As usual, she took her time answering. Couldn't she just sometimes say no?

His wish came true. "Go on," she finally answered. "I don't need anything. But be home in time for lunch, you hear?"

Ernest wheeled his bicycle out the door. Jack and Mike were popping wheelies on their bikes out front. Of course, Ernest couldn't do tricks like that. His bike weighed a few tons.

"Where are you headed with your truck?" Jack asked.

Across the street was Sonny the bike racer, sitting comfortably on his bike.

Ernest could just feel Mike's and Jack's eyes burning holes in his back. "Hey, you got your bike back together."

Getting a Coach

"I had to have the front wheel rebuilt and the derailleur straightened out. The rest was OK. I gotta go train. See you later." Sonny shot out on his bike like a rocket.

"Wait!" Ernest cried, but Sonny was gone.

"Who's that?" Mike called.

Ernest didn't answer. He jumped on his bike. He bent down low, his face close to the handlebars. He pictured the way Sonny looked on his bike. Then Ernest pushed out as fast as he could go. He felt more like a slug than a rocket. Still, he kept riding as hard as he could. After about three blocks, he was so out of breath, he had to stop.

Ernest put a foot down on the sidewalk. It took him a full three minutes to catch his breath. This would never work. The Citywide Cup race was in two months. And it was ten miles long. He could hardly ride three blocks at a fast pace.

Ernest kicked his dumb bike. But right away he felt bad. It wasn't his bike's problem. He bent down and rubbed the place he kicked. Now he wished his grandma *had* given him a shopping list. There was nothing to do. Ernest rode around the block slowly a few times. Then he went home.

That evening Ernest pulled on his jacket after supper.

"Where're you going, Ernie?" asked Grandma.

"It's *Ernest*," he said with a long sigh. Why couldn't she get his name right? "I'm just going out for a few minutes."

"It'll be dark in an hour."

"I'll be back."

"You better be."

"You *better* be," Melissa called after him. Ernest *knew* he wasn't that dumb-acting when he was eight.

He slammed the door.

Then, knowing what his grandma had to say about slamming doors, he opened it again. "Sorry," he called to her.

Grandma had come out of the kitchen. Shaking her head, she looked Ernest over. "I don't know what's come over you, Ernie."

"Nothing, Grandma." He quietly shut the door and left.

Ernest walked slowly up the street. He turned onto the street where Sonny lived. He looked at the row of apartment buildings. The green one, he thought. Luckily, he'd found Sonny's last name in the newspaper. Sonny King. Ernest thought that name sounded a lot grander than his own. Maybe he was even related to Martin Luther King, Jr. His grandma would like that.

Delusions of grandeur!

He found the name King on a buzzer. He rang the apartment. Someone buzzed the door and he opened it. Ernest climbed to the fourth floor and knocked on apartment 402. Sonny opened the door.

Ernest put out his hand and said, "Hello. You may remember me. I'm Ernest Peterson the third."

Sonny shook his hand. He looked a little confused. "Yeah, I remember you. Look, I just got in from my training ride. So I have to shower and everything."

"It's OK, you don't smell that bad." Then Ernest realized that maybe that wasn't what Sonny meant, so he added, "I'll just take a minute of your time." Ernest tried to sound as old as he could.

"Well, uh, OK, come on in. But just for a second."

"I want to train for the Citywide Cup," Ernest said, sitting on Sonny's couch.

"And I need help. See, I've never raced. I thought maybe you could give me some tips."

"That's great you want to race. But, see, I'm real busy. I race most weekends. And I train on the weekend days I don't race, as well as every day after work."

"I thought maybe I could help you out. I could time you on a stopwatch, or something."

"Do you have a bike?" Sonny asked.

Ernest felt his insides turn over. His face grew hot. Of *course* he had a bike, and Sonny had seen it.

"I mean a *racing* bike," Sonny added.

"You said my bike was a perfectly good machine," Ernest reminded him.

"Well, sure," Sonny said. He looked as if he were trying to back out of something. "But the Citywide Cup is in two months. Even the juniors have been training for months, even years."

"Fine," Ernest said. He put out his hand to shake Sonny's again. "I understand. You aren't going to help. I'll have to train on my own."

Ernest turned and headed for the door. His ears almost wagged they wanted to be called back so much. When he got to the door, he turned. But Sonny just looked at him.

Finally Sonny said, "You're some kid!"

Ernest opened the door. He waited a minute, still wishing Sonny would change his mind. He didn't. Ernest left.

The next morning after church, Ernest began training. If he had to do it on his own, he would. Just wait until he took first place. Sonny King would wish he had helped out!

But after riding his yellow clunker for an hour, Ernest felt worse than ever. His legs ached. And he was the slowest cyclist on the road. If he was going to enter the City-wide Cup race, he needed help. That's all there was to it.

Ernest wheeled his bike back to Sonny King's apartment building. Someone was just coming out, so Ernest didn't have to push the buzzer. He caught the opened door and pushed his bike inside. Then he hauled it up the four flights of stairs.

Sonny looked annoyed when he opened the door. Ernest blurted, "I've come back, hoping you'll change your mind. I tried training by myself. But three other cyclists passed me up."

Ernest looked Sonny King in the eye and waited. Sonny sighed. "You make me feel bad with that hangdog look of yours." He glanced at his watch. "OK, OK," he said, giving in to a smile. "I have a couple of hours before I meet some friends to ride.

I'll run you through a few things."

"Thanks, Sonny!" Ernest yelled.

"Hey!" Sonny put his hands over his ears. "Keep it down." Sonny popped him on the back of the head.

Ernest smiled. "I promise I won't take up much of your time."

Sonny fixed up Ernest's bike. He put a water bottle cage on it and gave him an old water bottle. He tightened some nuts and oiled the chain. He helped Ernest cut off the streamers. They also took off the bell.

"Let's get rid of these baskets," Sonny said. He started taking one off.

Ernest watched for a minute. He had a sinking feeling inside. Finally, he said, "Uh, Sonny, I think we have to leave the baskets on."

"Why? They'll slow you down."

"I know, but see, my grandma put them on. I do her shopping."

"Oh."

"Maybe she'd understand," Ernest said in a small voice.

Sonny shook his head. "Maybe not. Tell you what, Ernest. I bet I can find a way to make the baskets come on and off easily. That way you'll have them when you need them."

"That'd be great! Thanks, Sonny."

"OK, listen to me," Sonny said when he'd finished with Ernest's bike. He put his hands on Ernest's shoulders and made him face him. "If I'm going to work with you, no messing around. This will be work. Are you still game?"

Ernest nodded.

"I want you to begin by riding an hour a day. I don't care how fast. But you mustn't stop pedaling. Stay in a low, easy gear. That way you'll build up your muscles much faster than if you try to push a harder gear. The key to building up your legs is how many times you pedal, not how hard. Got it?"

Ernest nodded again, not wanting to re-mind Sonny that his old bike didn't *have* gears.

"Next, I want you to warm up every day before riding. Stretch all your muscles. Once you pull or strain a muscle, only rest will heal it. And rest will take away from important training time. Is that clear?"

Ernest grinned.

"You'll probably find you get much hun-grier than usual. Stay away from candy and fried food. Sugar and fat don't help you much in biking. Bike racers eat high-energy foods like potatoes, rice, noodles, and bread. Fruit and vegetables, too. Are you still with me?"

Ernest didn't nod this time. "Uh, Sonny? How many vegetables do I have to eat?"

"Whatever your grandmother puts on your plate."

Now Ernest smiled. He had to eat those anyway. As long as it wasn't extra vegetables.

"Any more questions?" Sonny asked.

"I was wondering about my bike. Do you really think I could win a race on this big thing?"

Ernest saw the doubt pass over Sonny's face. But Sonny looked bright again in a moment. He said, "In bike racing, the body is much more important than the bike. You could have the lightest, prettiest bike in the race. But it wouldn't help a bit unless you trained well.

"So listen," Sonny continued. "Train as I said for two weeks. If you stick to the plan one hundred percent, come and see me then. But don't bother if you've not done what I said, OK?"

Ernest saw by Sonny's face that he never expected to see him again. This was his way of getting rid of him.

"Fine," Ernest said. He shook Sonny's hand and left.

4: The Practice Bike Race

For two weeks Ernest rode *two* hours a day. He ate mountains of potatoes, rice, noodles, and bread. He even had extra helpings of vegetables—just to show Sonny King. He peeled the fried skin off his chicken. And he didn't touch a piece of candy.

The change in his legs was almost unbelievable. The muscles popped out just above his knees. And his calves got harder.

Exactly two weeks after his meeting

with Sonny, Ernest knocked on his apartment door once again. He wore shorts. That way Sonny would see his muscles and know how much he'd been training.

"Hi," Sonny said, opening the door, "I was expecting you."

"You were?" Ernest thought he was going to surprise Sonny.

"Sure. I could tell you weren't the kind of kid who gives up easily."

Ernest laughed. "What next?" he asked.

"We're going for a training ride. Got your bike?"

"Sure." Ernest couldn't believe how his luck had turned around. Sonny King, the bike racer who made the newspapers, was taking him on a training ride.

On the street, Sonny said, "Listen up. When you ride fast, you want to keep your head bent down. See, if you sit up straight, you catch a lot of wind. That slows you down. But if you duck your head and keep your back flat, you are more streamlined. You cut right through the air. Try it."

Ernest rode around the block once in racing form.

"Good. Now follow me." Sonny took off at a fast speed. Ernest set out after him.

Sonny turned onto Ernest's block. Mike and Jack were throwing a football in the street. Ernest didn't even look up as he flew past them. He kept his eyes on Sonny's back. And he made sure he stayed in racing form.

They rode for two hours. They rode all over the city and through two parks. They even rode out of the city for a while on a narrow road.

Ernest's legs felt as if they would fall off. But there was no way he would slow down. He knew that Sonny was already going a lot slower than usual. Finally, they ended up on Sonny's street again.

Sweat poured off Ernest's face. He was

so hungry he could eat a horse. But he'd never felt better in his life.

"Next weekend there's a race for young beginners," Sonny said. "It'd be good practice. You should try at least one race before the Citywide Cup."

"I could probably win a race for beginners," Ernest said. "After all, I've been training for two weeks."

Sonny looked doubtful once again. Ernest thought, I showed him the first time. He'll see what I can do!

"The race is outside the city," Sonny said. "I don't have a race on Saturday. Ask your grandmother if you can go. I'll drive you out there."

The next evening Ernest thought he would die as he marched along behind his grandma. They were going to Sonny King's apartment.

"Never mind," he told her. "I changed my mind. I don't want to go to the race. Let's just go home."

But his grandma was determined. "Whether you go Saturday or not, I don't like you spending time with anyone I haven't met."

"And grilled," Ernest mumbled, but not loud enough for her to hear.

When Sonny King opened the door, Ernest's grandma said, "My boy says you're going to drive him to a bike race Saturday?"

"Yes, ma'am," Sonny said, nodding. Ernest's grandma was giving him the once-over, from head to toe. Then she began her questions. Who do you live with? Where do you work? Who is your mama? Ernest could see her looking over Sonny's shoulder, too, checking out his apartment. He knew she was even inspecting the rug to see if he vacuumed regularly. She was that particular.

Ernest had begged his grandma a hundred times not to give his friends the third degree like this. She even did it to his teachers. But his grandma would answer, "Ernie, I already lost your mama and papa. And I know they're in heaven watching how I raise you and your sister. I aim to do a good job. If there's one thing that I want to do in this life, it's see that you and Melissa have a safe passage through childhood. There are just too many kooks—"

"OK, OK, Grandma." Once she'd gotten to this particular lecture, it was very hard to get her to stop.

Apparently, Sonny King passed the test, because she decided Ernest could go to the bike race.

In the car on Saturday, Ernest asked Sonny, "Do you think you'll win the City-wide Cup?"

"No. There're a lot of fast bikers in this city. I've placed second or third, but have never won a race, Ernest."

"You have to believe in yourself!" Ernest

cried. He made his hand into a fist and hit the other open hand. "That's what my teachers in school always say."

"They're probably right. But you also have to be reasonable. I'm not as fast as some of those guys."

"So who's faster than you in this city?" Ernest found it hard to believe that anyone could be faster than Sonny King.

"There's Tiger Jones for one. He's not only fast, he's mean. That's one thing you have to watch out for. Most racers are fair. There're always a few, though, who will try to mess you up. I've seen guys stick their bike pumps in another guy's wheels. Things like that do happen. Just keep your eyes open when you're racing today. Stay away from racers who aren't riding a straight line."

As Ernest lifted his bike off Sonny's car, he saw other boys pointing. Several of them started laughing at his bike.

Most of the boys had on all the cool bike

(44)

clothes, too. Ernest wore his usual shorts and an old helmet of Sonny's.

Ernest threw his chin in the air. Let them laugh, he'd show them. Didn't Sonny say the body was much more important than the bike? Certainly Sonny knew better than these beginners.

"Good luck," Sonny told him. "Remember, draft the pack for as long as you can. Make the front riders do the work."

"Sure, I know," Ernest said. He rolled his bike up to the starting line. His ears pounded and his hands shook. He threw a leg over his bike and looked to the man with the starting gun.

Gray clouds gathered in the sky. A light rain began to fall. Ernest was cold in his shorts. A few of the other boys pulled on racing tights.

Ernest looked quickly at Sonny. He gave him the thumbs-up sign. Ernest felt brave again.

The starting gun broke the silence.

Ernest pulled out fast. He stood up and pedaled hard. One lap passed, and then two. Ernest was doing fine. He stayed in back of the first group.

He remembered what Sonny said about racing in a group. "Stay in back of the pack at first. That way they cut through the wind for you. It's much easier pedaling with someone else doing the hard part out front. That's called drafting."

So Ernest stayed in back. He drafted the other bikers. The race was ten laps long. On the last lap, near the finish line, he would break free.

The cold wind whistled past Ernest's face. A light rain continued to fall. Ernest started to feel his legs grow heavier. He started to fall behind. The pack pulled farther and farther ahead. Ernest was left behind with a few other boys.

Then something snapped in Ernest's leg. A sharp pain shot up the leg. Ernest wanted to pull over and stop. But he kept riding. And he stayed in racing form even though it hurt his neck.

Then the worst thing happened. Ernest heard a loud blast. He thought someone had shot a gun. He looked around quickly.

But then his bike started bumping unevenly along the road. He had to hold on tight to keep from crashing. His bike was swinging back and forth.

"Watch out!" a racer yelled flying past him.

"Get off the road!" another shouted.

Ernest realized his front tire had blown out. He worked the bike off the road and stopped.

Driving home in the car, Sonny said, "Don't take it too hard. This was your first race. You couldn't help the flat tire. And that pulled muscle was just bad luck."

Ernest rubbed his hurt leg. He didn't feel like talking at all.

"When you get home, I want you to ice that leg. Ice takes down the swelling. See,

(47)

all the blood rushes to the hurt place. That's good. The blood feeds the area. But the blood also causes you to hurt. It's like filling a balloon too much. Ice will take down the swelling.

"I also want you to take two ibuprofen every four hours. Just like it says on the bottle. That will take down the swelling, too. And rest. Nothing will help more than rest. Get plenty of sleep and stay off the bike for a week."

"A week! Sonny, I have to train for the Citywide Cup."

"You won't be riding the rest of the summer unless you take care of your pulled muscle now. Believe me. I shouldn't have let you ride in this cold weather in shorts. You need some biking tights."

Ernest was silent. Where was he going to get biking tights?

Finally, Ernest said, "I pulled a muscle. And I got a flat. But you know, Sonny, I was falling way behind before those things

(49)

happened. They aren't excuses for my not doing well. Let's face it."

Sonny didn't say anything.

"I'm going to have to train a lot harder for the Citywide Cup."

Sonny looked surprised. "I don't know, Ernest. Unless you get another bike . . . "

"You said—"

"I know what I said. And it's true. It's just that the Citywide Cup is a much bigger race. The boys in it have been training all summer, maybe for a few years."

Ernest crossed his arms and stayed silent for a few minutes. He was tired of Sonny always doubting things. Then he said, "How can I get a good racing bike if I don't win the Citywide Cup?"

"Just don't get your hopes up so high."

Ernest looked at Sonny. "Sonny, it might help you if you got *your* hopes up a little higher. You're always saying you won't win. You're always saying things aren't possible. I bet *you* will win the City-wide Cup."

"Thanks, pal. You're probably right about shooting for the stars. It's better than setting your sights too low. But as for me winning the Citywide Cup? Not a chance."

Ernest just shook his head. Sonny was almost as practical as his grandma.

5: Bad News at Dinner

"**Y**ou look funny," Ernest told Sonny when he opened the door. Sonny had come to dinner wearing a suit and tie.

Last week Ernest's grandma had said, "I don't like you driving around with a stranger."

"He's not a stranger, Grandma. He's Sonny King, my coach. You've met him yourself, remember? You said he was OK."

"If he's not a stranger, then you better

have him to dinner so I can get to know him better."

So here was Sonny all dressed up. Ernest realized he shouldn't have said he looked funny. The words just flew out of his mouth.

"Thanks, Ernest," Sonny said straightening his tie. "You look smashing yourself."

Melissa came out of her room carrying Sniffy who barked at Sonny. Ernest crossed his fingers Melissa wouldn't say anything dumb.

"Ernest thinks he's going to be a bike racer," she told Sonny right away. "But Mike and Jack, his friends, say it's a joke."

"Be quiet, Melissa," Ernest growled under his breath. His grandma didn't like him to tell his sister to be quiet. But right now he had to.

"And besides," Melissa continued, "Ernest is too skinny to do any sports at all. That's what his football coach said."

(53)

Ernest's grandma handed Sonny a glass of ice tea. "Mind yourself, Melissa," she warned.

Ernest wanted to kick his sister. His football coach did say that. And nothing had ever made him angrier. He dropped off the football team after that. He never got to play, anyway.

"Well, football is a whole different sport than bike racing," Sonny said. "Think about it. For football you have to be big because you get knocked around. The point is to stay on your feet.

"But in biking, you want to be as light as possible. The heavier you are, the harder you have to work. It's the difference between walking with a heavy suitcase or a light one. Which way could you go faster? With the light one, of course.

"Your brother has the perfect build for bike racing," Sonny told Melissa.

Ernest was too old to say, "So there!" But he sure felt like it.

(54)

"Tell me," Sonny said, changing the subject, "how's your pulled muscle?"

"It's much better. I think I can start training again. I did just what you told me. I've been icing it on and off. And I've been taking ibuprofen."

"Great," Sonny said. "It'd be really good if you could get some riding tights. They would keep your legs warmer. You'd have much less chance of getting hurt."

Ernest nodded, knowing there was no money for riding tights. Already his grandma had said he and Melissa would have to start school this year in last year's clothes. She'd spent all her extra money on his yellow bike. . . .

At least Ernest could tell his grandma liked Sonny. He could tell by the way she nodded and raised her chin at him. He spoke nicely and said "please" and "thank you" a lot. Those words went a long way with Ernest's grandma.

Ernest breathed easier now. His

(55)

grandma would let him continue training with Sonny.

At the end of dinner, Sonny said, "I have a little bad news for you, Ernest."

Ernest didn't like the sound of his voice.

"I won't be able to make it to your City-wide Cup race in two weeks. They've scheduled the juniors' race at the same time as the adult men's race. And the two races are in different places."

Suddenly Ernest's dinner felt like a rock inside of him. His hands felt cold. Without Sonny there, Ernest would not feel so brave about the other boys laughing at his bike.

"That's OK," Ernest said, "I can go on my own."

Sonny looked at Ernest's grandma. "There's still a problem. How can Ernest get to the race?"

A long silence filled the room.

Sonny said, "You don't drive do you, ma'am?" Ernest's grandma shook her head.

(57)

"I'll ride my bike," Ernest said in his most manly voice.

"The race is out of town," Sonny said softly. "It's twenty miles from here. On the freeway. I'm really sorry, pal."

Ernest looked at his grandma. She just kept taking bites and swallowing. She acted as if she hadn't heard a thing.

After another long silence, Melissa said, "You might as well quit training, then, because you're not going to the race."

"Oh, be quiet." Ernest might have broken into tears and run to his room except for Sonny.

For once his grandma didn't scold him. She said, "I told you, Melissa, mind yourself."

The blackberry pie made Ernest feel a little better. No one made blackberry pie like his grandma. Besides, he knew she made it special for his friend. Still, without the race to look forward to, the summer would stretch on forever.

Bad News at Dinner

Ernest walked Sonny down to the street.

"I'm sorry about the race," Sonny said.

Ernest put his hands on his hips. He looked out over the skyline and bit his lip. "It's OK."

"If there was any way I could take you, you know I would."

"Sure," Ernest said. "But I think I'll keep training even if I can't try for that racing bike in the Citywide Cup. I'm kind of hooked on biking, anyway."

Sonny smiled and put an arm around Ernest. "I have a race on Saturday. Maybe you'd like to come watch."

"That'd be great." Ernest smiled.

"OK. Ask your grandma. If she says yes, I'll pick you up at eight on Saturday morning."

6: Sonny King's Race

Ernest decided he was going to coach Sonny. He figured that if he couldn't race in the Citywide Cup, at least he could see to it that Sonny won. Of course, Ernest wouldn't tell Sonny he was going to coach him. He would have to be kind of secretive about it.

Ernest prepared all kinds of talks in his head for Sonny. He practiced in front of his mirror.

"Sonny, you have to say 'Yes!' to yourself. How can you win without *thinking* you can win?"

Ernest knew that Sonny worked hard, but he didn't think he had the right attitude. You had to think positively in order to win.

On Saturday, Ernest rose at five in the morning. He'd be gone most of the day at Sonny's race. So he had to do his training ride before he left. By the time he ate his breakfast and dressed, the sun had risen. Ernest pushed his yellow clunker out to the street.

The city was quiet at that hour. Ernest rode fast. He pushed the bike as hard as he could. The wind blasted him in the face. The street disappeared beneath his wheels.

Sometimes, Ernest forgot he was on a big heavy bike. He imagined he rode a racing bike that was as light as a feather. He imagined that he rode in a pack of full-grown racers, like Sonny.

He pictured himself pushing to the front

(61)

of the pack. The wind hissed past his ears. He went so fast his bike almost left the ground. Fans screamed as he crossed the finish line in first place.

Then Ernest would snap back to reality. More delusions of grandeur.

At home Ernest showered. He ate twelve hotcakes, his second breakfast. Sonny arrived right at eight.

At the race, Sonny warmed up. He stretched and spun around the block a few times on his bike. Ernest watched all the bikers carefully.

Before the race started, Sonny pointed out Tiger Jones. He was a thick man with a lot of hair on his arms. Sonny had said he could be mean in a pack. Ernest believed it by the looks of him.

Finally, all the racers pulled up to the starting line. The race would circle a shopping center twenty-five times.

Ernest edged up to Sonny. He said in a low voice, "Shoot for the stars, Sonny."

"Thanks, pal," Sonny said. Ernest backed up to where the other fans stood.

The race began.

Sonny's face looked set. He pedaled evenly, smoothly. Ernest crossed his fingers. He wanted Sonny to win more than anything.

The pack went around and around. A few riders fell off the back of the pack. Sonny stayed with the front group, but he kept to the back of it. Ernest knew he was drafting the pack. He wondered when Sonny would pull to the front.

Ernest decided to cross the parking lot to the other side of the shopping center. There were fewer fans over there. He could get a better look at the racers as they went around.

He got to the other side of the course just as the pack rounded the corner. Ernest spotted Sonny. Very close to his side rode Tiger Jones. Both men were riding hard, trying for the front place.

Just as they rode past, Ernest saw Tiger Jones say something to Sonny. Then Tiger jerked his bike a little toward Sonny. Sonny panicked and swerved. His bike tipped and he almost crashed. Then he managed to pull his bike back in line. But Tiger was out front.

Ernest couldn't believe anyone would be that bad a sport. He knew Tiger wouldn't have done that in front of all the people at the finish line. Ernest ran back to the finish line to watch the end of the race.

He waited with the rest of the fans to see the last lap. Here they came!

Good! thought Ernest. Sonny had pulled back up even with Tiger. Sonny, Tiger, and another racer led the pack. They were neck and neck.

They swiftly drew closer to the finish line. Twenty yards, ten yards, five yards. Sonny rose off the seat of his bike. He

leaned forward and started to pull ahead. Ernest could hear Tiger growling like an animal. That must be how he got his name, he thought.

"Go, Sonny!" Ernest yelled. He was only inches ahead of Tiger and the other man.

At the last second, Tiger yanked his bike ahead. As he passed Sonny, he swerved into him to throw him off. Sonny pulled aside. He lost a very important second. The other racer passed Sonny, too.

Tiger finished first, the other man second, and Sonny third.

Ernest knew enough to keep his mouth shut going home in the car. Sonny's own mouth was set in a tight angry line. He kept saying, "And I almost had it!"

"Tiger was playing dirty," Ernest finally said. "I saw him."

"In bike racing you have to be able to take that. There're always guys like Tiger Jones. I blew it when I let his swerving get me. I should have held my line."

(66)

"Next time," Ernest said. "Besides, look at the good side. You came in third. Which puts you ahead of about thirty other guys."

Sonny looked at him and smiled for the first time in over an hour. "Who's coaching who around here?"

"You get too down on yourself," Ernest continued. "You have to think positively."

"That's not a problem you have," Sonny joked. "But thanks, pal."

7: Two Surprises

The Citywide Cup race took place in one week. Ernest invited Mike and Jack over to watch it on TV. They hadn't been making fun of him lately. Even those jokers felt bad when they heard Ernest couldn't go to the Citywide Cup.

Two days before the race, Ernest's grandma came home from downtown. She handed a paper bag to Ernest saying, "Don't show your sister. She'll want something, too."

(68)

Two Surprises

Ernest opened the bag. Inside he found a beautiful pair of biking tights. They were black with a bright blue stripe down each leg.

"Grandma!" he yelled running into the kitchen. "Grandma, thanks!"

"Didn't I tell you to keep it quiet?" she asked, acting all businesslike. She began popping string beans and throwing them in a pot. Not a smile, but she couldn't fool Ernest. He kissed her on the cheek.

"Child, you don't even have to get up on your toes to do that anymore," she said, shaking her head. It was true. Ernest seemed to have grown a foot this summer. He was not that much shorter than Sonny.

"What are you thanking Grandma for?" Melissa came trotting around the corner.

His grandma gave Ernest a "Didn't I tell you?" look.

Ernest said, "I'm thanking her for making string beans. My favorite vegetable."

"But you don't like vegetables . . . " Me-

lissa called as Ernest skipped out of the kitchen.

That night Ernest's grandma came into his room. She said, "Let me see that story you clipped out of the newspaper."

Ernest had pinned the Citywide Cup story up on his wall. He took it down and handed it to her. His grandma put a hand on her hip and read the clipping. She shook her head and left the room.

Ernest thought he knew why she wanted to read the newspaper story. She was angry with him for wanting to be in the race. She saw that he just wanted to win that racing bike. Ernest knew he'd hurt her feelings. She probably thought he was the most self-ish boy in the world. But he couldn't help it. He *did* want that racing bike.

The next morning Ernest pulled on his new bike tights. He couldn't believe how good-looking they were. He tightened his leg muscles and watched the blue stripe move around.

"You look like a girl!" Melissa screamed when he came out of his room. "What are you doing, taking dancing lessons?"

Ernest felt his full ten years this morning, so he didn't respond to her baiting. He bent down and petted Sniffy. Then he asked, "Where's Grandma?"

"She's been on the telephone in there for half an hour," Melissa said, pointing at the closed door of their grandma's bedroom.

It wasn't like their grandma to talk on the telephone behind a closed door. Both Ernest and Melissa stood looking at the door. Just then their grandma came out.

"Well, what are you two doing?" she asked in a huff.

"We weren't listening," Melissa said.

Ernest thought, Melissa makes it sound as if we *were* listening.

"You better get out on that bike," Ernest's grandma said. She pointed to his new tights. "And warm up good."

Two Surprises

Ernest looked confused. Why all of a sudden was she so pushy about his bike riding?

"I've been calling cab companies all morning," she said, throwing on the kitchen light. Before she said another word, she got out the flour and sugar. Melissa and Ernest stood openmouthed waiting to hear what she was up to. "I've found one that will take your bike in the trunk. All three of us will go on Saturday to the race."

"Grandma!"

"Go on, get on that bike. I don't want to go to all this trouble and money for nothing. Get riding!" She hit him on the behind.

"Go on," Melissa squealed. She also hit him on the behind. "Get riding!"

On Saturday morning the Peterson family got up at six o'clock. Ernest's grandma made hot cereal and eggs and toast for Ernest. He needed to load up on high-energy foods.

"Do you think the bike will really fit in the cab's trunk?" Ernest asked at least three times.

"We'll see," his grandma kept answering.

At quarter to seven, Melissa and his grandma were ready. Ernest was a little embarrassed. They both wore their Sunday dresses. He was sure the other racers' friends and families would be in sweats or jeans. But of course he didn't say anything. His grandma and even Melissa were giving up a lot to pay for a cab to his race. Ernest just hoped he won to make it worth it.

At seven the cab came. The bike fit easily in the trunk. They used a little string to tie the trunk lid down.

The ride out to the racecourse took forever. Ernest kept asking what time it was. His grandma stopped answering him after the third time. For once, Melissa was quiet.

8: The Citywide Cup Race

Finally, they arrived at the race. The course was ten times around a lake, ten miles.

Ernest swallowed his shy feelings as they pulled up. So what if everyone didn't come with their bikes in the trunks of cabs! So what if everyone didn't bring their grandmas and little sisters wearing their church clothes! So what if everyone didn't have big, clunky yellow bikes!

None of that would stop Ernest. He'd

show them by being the fastest ten-year-old racer around.

Ernest did wish Sonny were here, though.

The day was turning out to be clear and blue. The early morning sun poured down on his back. Later today he knew it would be hot and sticky. By then, Ernest expected to be the proud owner of a new racing bike.

After warming up, Ernest kissed his grandma—and even Melissa. Then he rolled his bike to the starting line.

"Stand back," a tall boy told Ernest. He pushed in front of Ernest.

"What are you doing? I had this place," Ernest told him. He tried to work his way back in front of the boy, but the boy's father came up and blocked his way. The father began talking to his son and wouldn't let Ernest through.

Oh, well, Ernest thought. The race is ten miles. What difference does it make where I start?

The Citywide Cup Race

"That's some bike you have there," said another boy on the starting line.

Ernest looked up quickly. He was ready to snap back a sharp reply. He figured this boy was also making fun of him. But the redheaded boy only looked interested, not mean.

"Well, it's what I got," Ernest said with a weak smile. He wouldn't let these boys shake his will to win.

"Good luck," the boy said.

"Thanks," Ernest said. At least there was one other good sport out here.

"Everyone on your marks!" cried the woman starting the race. "Get set!" The gun fired. Ernest took one quick look at his grandma and Melissa. Both stood on their tiptoes to see him. His grandma had her hands locked in front of her chest. She looked as if she was more nervous than he was. At the last second Melissa screamed, "Go, Ernie!"

"*Ernest*," he whispered to himself. He

pushed forward, riding in the middle of the pack. Suddenly, he felt pretty glad his family dressed up for his race. That meant they thought it was important.

Sweat ran down Ernest's face. He stayed in the middle of the pack just like Sonny said. Later, he'd have to pull ahead.

"Get that piece of junk out of my way," a voice snarled in back of Ernest. The rider pulled up by his side. Ernest saw it was the same tall boy who pushed ahead of him at the starting line.

Ernest looked straight ahead and didn't answer.

"You hear me?" the boy said. "You're in my way. Kid, this is the Citywide Cup. A *bike* race. Not a go-cart race."

Ernest realized that his big bike took up a lot of space. If he moved, he would open up a path to the front of the pack. This tall kid thought he could make Ernest move.

Then Ernest had an idea. They'd ridden about three miles. This was far too soon to break ahead of the pack. He should let this boy go ahead. He'd only tire himself out. At least Ernest could get rid of him.

Ernest moved a little to the right.

"Sucker!" the boy called as he rose out of his seat. He pumped ahead to the front of the pack. Then he broke free of the pack. The boy was taking the lead.

As Ernest raced around the lake, he enjoyed the scenery. The sun sparkled on the water. The trees whispered as he rode, "Hang in there, you can do it."

Ernest knew he'd trained well. Even with his heavy bike, he kept up with the other racers. On the last lap, he would break to the front.

Two laps later, Ernest saw the tall boy up ahead. Ernest smiled to himself even as he gasped for air and continued pedaling. The pack was gaining on the tall boy. He'd tried to break ahead way too soon.

The tall boy madly swung his bike back and forth. He looked all worn out. He

(79)

moved slower and slower. Soon the pack swallowed him up.

As Ernest passed him, he wished he wasn't such a nice guy. He'd have liked to have a short word with that creep. But he kept his mind on his racing form. He didn't have time for kids who were full of themselves. The racers flew around and around the lake. Each time Ernest passed the starting point he heard Melissa yell, "Grandma! There he is! That's Ernie!"

Then on the seventh time around, he even heard his grandma. Her loud, deep voice boomed out, "Go ahead, Ernest! Move on out!"

She even got his name right.

On the eighth lap, a group of about five boys broke ahead of the pack. Ernest decided to go with them. He rose off his seat and took off.

For a few seconds he felt wonderful. What a great feeling to leave all those other guys behind!

(80)

But then he realized just how fast this group of five really was. These boys were *fast*.

Ernest struggled to keep up. But he started to fall behind. He also became very, very tired. In a matter of minutes, he found himself back with the main pack. But he'd used too much energy trying to keep up with that small fast group. Rider after rider passed Ernest. He fell farther and farther behind.

Ernest felt tears rising up in his chest. He shook his head hard and tried to pedal faster. He just couldn't do it. Even the big group was far ahead of him now.

Ernest had one more lap to finish the race. He, and the few others who hadn't kept up, pushed on. He realized that he wasn't going to win that racing bike.

Ernest crossed the finish line in thirtieth place. His grandma and Melissa rushed over to him. "Well," his grandma said, pointing at the few boys still coming in behind Ernest, "you're not the last."

"Thanks, Grandma," Ernest said sourly, "that's just great."

"Chin up," his grandma said. Always, always practical. Couldn't she understand he wanted to *win*?

But Ernest did put up his chin when he saw a boy wheeling his bike toward him. It was the nice redheaded boy he'd met on the starting line.

"You did great on that heavy bike," the boy said. "You must have pretty strong legs to pull a bike that heavy so fast."

"How'd you do?" Ernest asked.

"Second place," the boy said.

"Congratulations," Ernest said. He shook the boy's hand. "Maybe I'll see you next time."

"Next time?" Melissa piped in. "Don't tell me you're doing this *again*? But you didn't win!"

"Enough out of you," their grandma said. Then, "Will you look who's coming!"

(82)

Running toward them was Sonny King, the last person Ernest wanted to see. Sonny still had on his bike clothes and he was grinning from ear to ear.

Ernest wished he never had to see Sonny again. How could he tell him how poorly he did?

Ernest took a deep breath and marched toward Sonny. To get it over with, before Sonny could say a word Ernest said, "I blew it, Sonny. I'm sorry. I took thirtieth place."

Ernest tried hard to look Sonny in the eye.

"Never mind," Sonny said, slapping Ernest on the back.

How could he be so light about Ernest's loss?

Sonny said, "Don't you want to hear how I did?"

"Sure." Ernest couldn't smile, though.

"First place."

Ernest was floored. "You're kidding!

(83)

Sonny, that's perfect! That's great! Oh, boy!"

Ernest danced all around Sonny. Sonny won the Citywide Cup! Suddenly, Ernest could forget all about his own race. After all, he'd have a lot more chances.

"Come on," Sonny said. "There's no time. I came to get the three of you. I have a meeting with the press in less than an hour. Come along, and then I'll take you all home."

"Good," said practical Grandma, "that'll save us the cab fare."

They quickly put Ernest's clunker on the bike rack on top of Sonny's car and jumped in. Sonny drove back to the course where his own race had taken place. He parked and helped Ernest's grandma out of the car.

They all hurried to the far side of the parking lot where the press conference would take place. There was a raised platform with several mikes set up on it. Er-

(84)

nest saw that at least two TV stations were present.

"There he is," called a man from a newspaper. "Come on up here, Sonny King."

A woman rushed up to him. A TV camera pointed at Sonny, Ernest, Melissa, and Grandma. The woman said, "Good afternoon, we have with us today the winner of the Citywide Cup bike race—Mr. Sonny King!"

The TV camera followed Sonny's every move.

Sonny took Ernest's arm. "Come on with me."

"What?" Ernest held back.

"I said, come on, boy! Let's go."

Ernest followed Sonny up onto the raised platform. Someone pushed mikes in their faces. The news reporters pushed in closely.

"Sonny King, you've placed in several races in the last couple years, but never pulled off a win. How do you feel about

(85)

taking first place in the Citywide Cup?" asked a newspaper reporter.

"Great. What can I say? I was dying to win this race."

Ernest felt kind of stupid standing there. But then he remembered that Mike and Jack would be watching. He was on TV with Sonny King, winner of the Citywide Cup! He threw back his shoulders.

"You know you've just won a new top-of-the-line bicycle," a TV reporter said. "What do you plan to do with your old racer, Sonny?"

Sonny smiled and threw an arm around Ernest. "I'd like everyone to meet my friend, Mr. Ernest Peterson the third." Sonny lifted Ernest's hand over his head, just as if *he* were a winner. "In a few years, I expect him to be one of the finest racers in this country. He's taught me a lot about believing in myself and shooting for the stars. For that, I'd like to

(87)

give my old racing bike to Mr. Ernest Peterson the third."

Ernest thought he might fly to pieces from happiness right there on TV. He, Ernest Peterson, would be training on Sonny King's old bike! The world could have stopped in that moment, and Ernest would have died very, very happy.

Driving home in the car, Sonny told them about every inch of his race. Ernest listened carefully. Then he told Sonny all about his own race.

Ernest could hardly get his mind off his new bike. It rode on top of the car right now. It was a little big, but Sonny said he could fix it up to fit Ernest pretty well. Besides, Ernest was growing fast. He worried, though, that his grandma read his thoughts about being so happy to have the new bike.

Finally, Ernest said, "Grandma, you

know I really love the bike you gave me. I like both bikes the same."

"Don't lie to me, son," she said sharply. "And speaking of lies."

Ernest winced. He knew what was coming.

"What's this Ernest Peterson *the third* all about?"

Ernest searched his mind for an answer. He never thought about Sonny saying that on TV! But then his grandma just chuckled and squeezed his knee.

"Ernie," she began.

He cut in: "Ernest."

"Ernest," she said. "About that new bike. I don't think you wanted the racing bike as much as you wanted to work hard at something and win. You deserve the new bike. But maybe you needed that old heavy bike to get you started. Look where you are now! You have a coach, a new bike, and a couple of races under your belt. That old bike started you off very nicely."

(89)

Ernest sat quietly in the car for a moment. He looked at the back of Sonny's head. Then he said, "Yes, Grandma, that yellow bike is a perfectly good machine."